David, We're PREGNANT!

101 cartoons for
Expecting Parents
by Lynn Johnston

 Meadowbrook

Distributed by Simon and Schuster
New York

Meadowbrook Press Edition
88   20   19

PRINTED IN THE UNITED STATES OF AMERICA

Library of Congress Catalog Number: 77-82214

ISBN 0-915658-04-6
S & S Ordering #: 0-671-54476-4

Copyright   © 1975 by Potlatch Publications

Published by Meadowbrook, Inc., Deephaven,
MN 55391

BOOK TRADE DISTRIBUTION by Simon and
Schuster, a division of Simon & Schuster, Inc.,
1230 Avenue of the Americas, New York, NY
10020

Once upon a time there were no cartoons on the ceiling of my examining room.

From my point of view, of course, the examining room was always an interesting place where I met fascinating people, with perplexing problems for me to solve. The relationship was simple and direct. The patients had questions. I had gone to medical school and learned answers. The examining room was the place where the questions and the answers got together. Both patient and doctor went in for the same purpose, and both went out satisfied.

One day a perceptive woman, who had lain all too long on the table counting the dots on an otherwise blank ceiling, asked me why I didn't put any pictures up there. I didn't have a good answer, but I realized it was a good question. And I was struck with the realization that the patient's point of view from the examining table was very different from the doctor's point of view. A host of new questions started to crowd in.

When does pregnancy really begin? Is it, like we were taught in school, at the precise moment when sperm and egg join together, or is it earlier, when a couple start to plan and yearn for a family? Or is it perhaps later, with the realization of pregnancy, and the growing awareness of the life within?

What is pregnancy? Is it the weight gains and the blood pressures and the morning sicknesses and the strange symptoms the doctor sees? Or is it the hopes and fears, and joys and tremblings, and a new body to adjust to, and a new shape to learn to love? Is it a time for parents to prepare for their new exciting role to come?

What are prenatal classes? A passing fad to keep patients occupied? Or an opportunity for us to learn about our bodies and ourselves, to learn the skills needed for the awesome task ahead?

What is labor? Is it a series of uterine contractions working to dilate the cervix and expel a new baby into the world? Or is it a dreaded yet anticipated experience, unknown and unknowable, through which one must pass with only old wives' tales and untested prenatal classes as uncertain guides?

Indeed, what is the new baby? A little patient to be weighed and tested, and formulas to be adjusted? Or a new individual who will change lovers into parents, and mates into a family, with new joys and sleepless nights?

There are many books about pregnancy, but most are written from the professional's point of view. The patient's answers to these questions are rarely expressed. In this book, Lynn has given the parents' viewpoint, clearly and pointedly. For parents, for parents-to-be, and for professionals too.

And now I have cartoons on my ceiling.

MURRAY W. ENKIN, M.D.

Don't be so depressed..... Remember when getting your period was a good sign?
LYNN

I'm pretty sure that I am....
but what if I'm not.... what if
it's negative ... or nerves... or
imagination. Actually, I'm
positive I am. I'll phone
for a checkup. But what
if they tell me I'm not....
better wait another week
to make sure ..... No. Why
wait if I'm POSITIVE! ...
Then again... what if I'm not....
On the other hand...
maybe ...,.....

Lynn

19

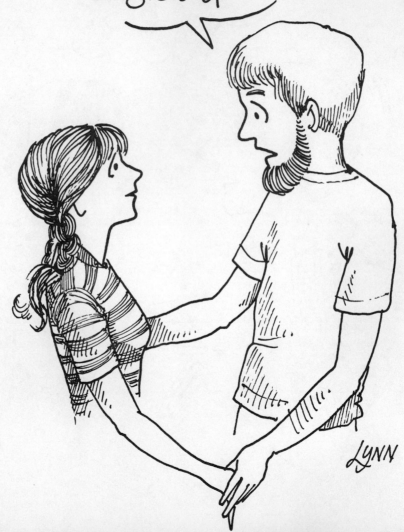

25

I don't understand it, Dad... Jan just found out she's pregnant—but I'm the one with the knots in my stomach!

Well, congratulations, Elly! .....
You know, Lewis & I would have had children...but, we just don't have the patience.
LYNN

31

33

35

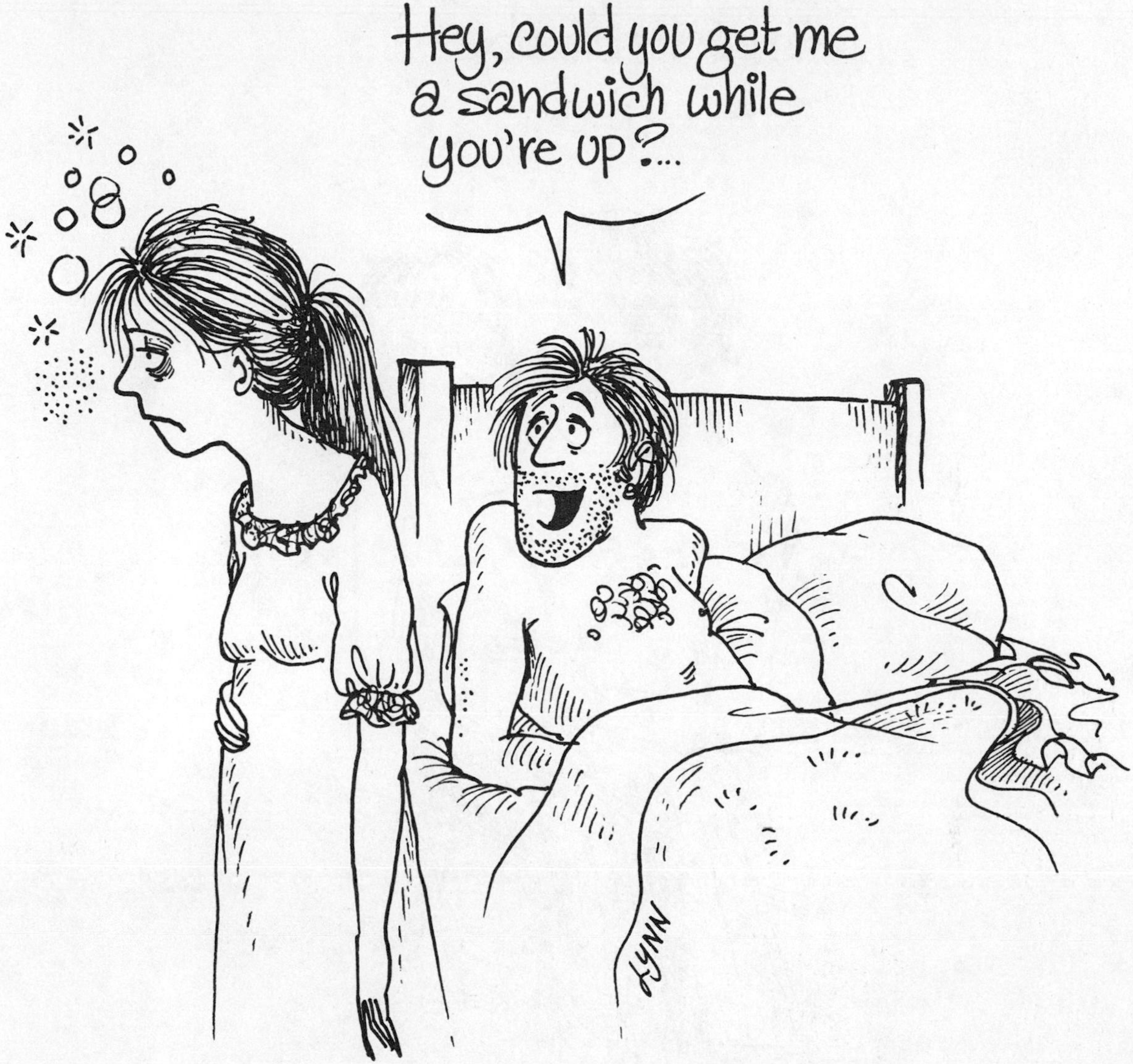
Hey, could you get me a sandwich while you're up?...
LYNN

40

41

48

51

53

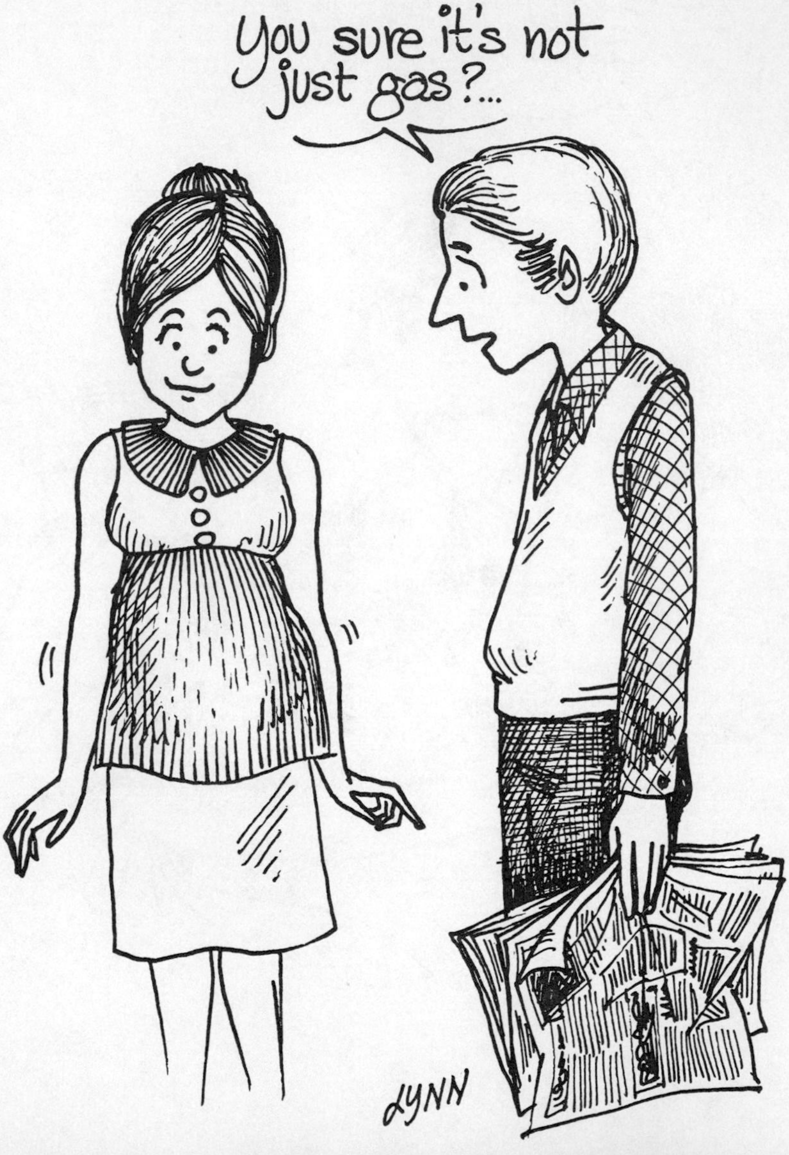
You sure it's not just gas?...
LYNN

Mom, Ken's agreed to go to prenatal classes with Barbie....

THE LAMAZE METHOD

Lynn

57

58

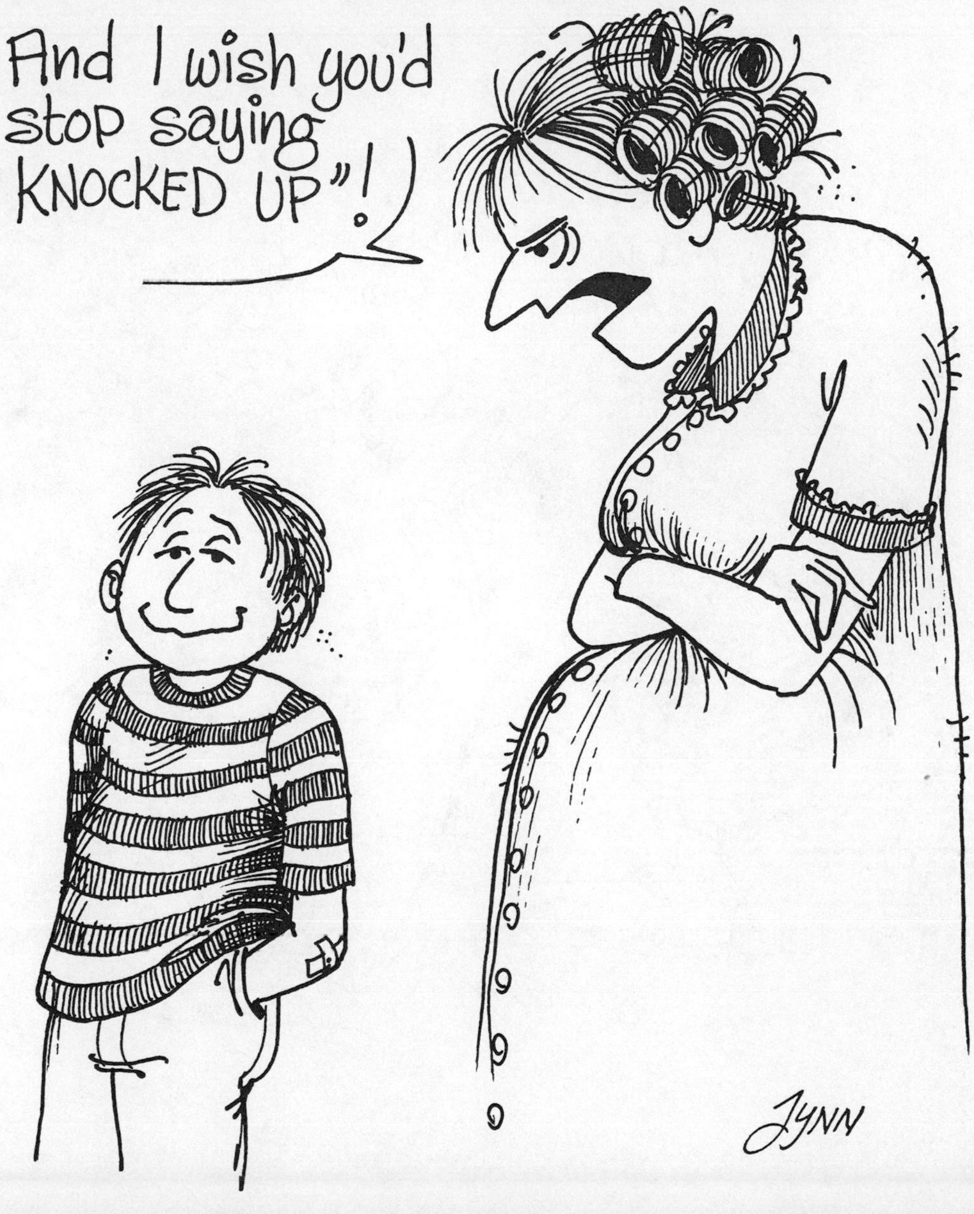
And I wish you'd stop saying "KNOCKED UP"!
LYNN

62

64

While you're waddling around town- could you pick me up a copy of the evening edition?
LYNN

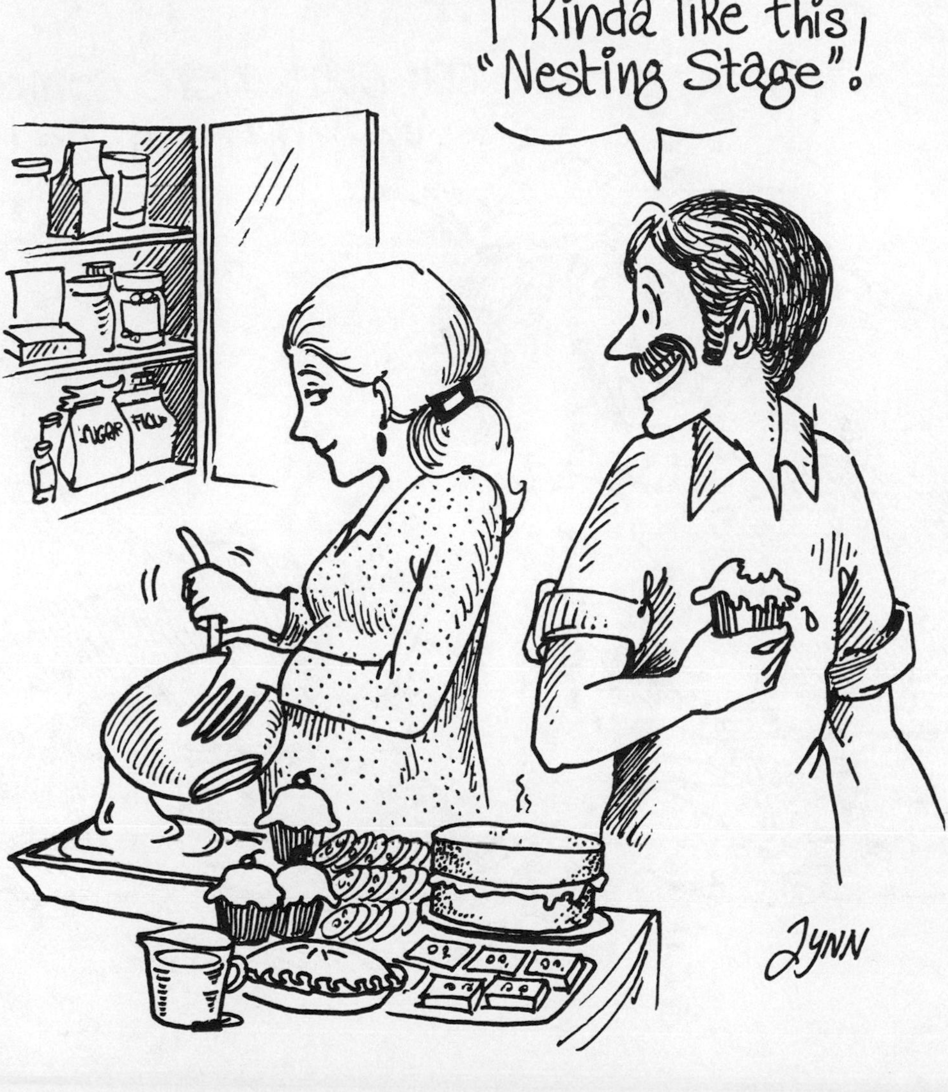
I Kinda like this "Nesting Stage"!
LYNN

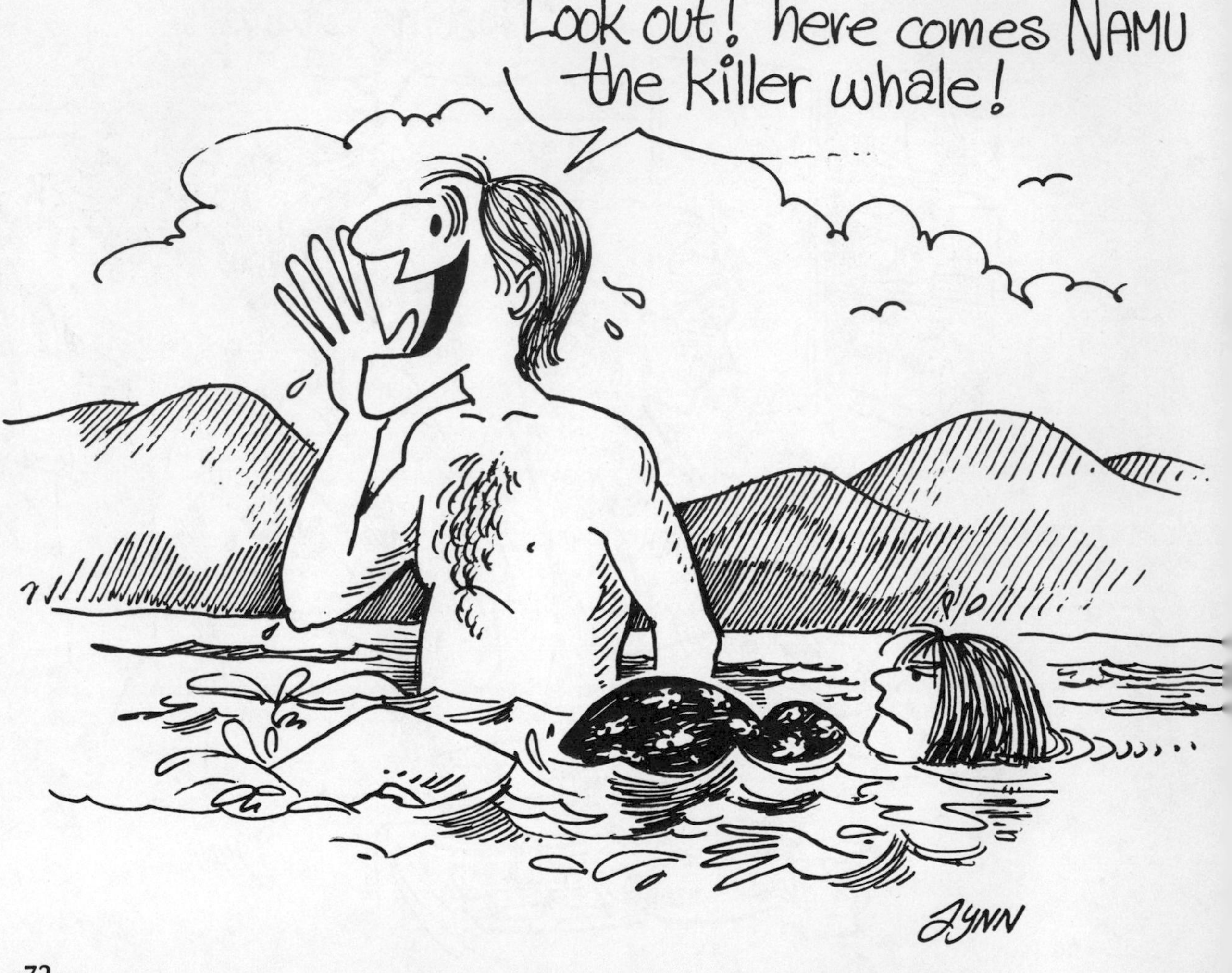
Look out! here comes NAMU the killer whale!
LYNN

73

No matter how I lie, I'm uncomfortable....
I think I'm going to have to learn
how to sleep standing up.

Lynn

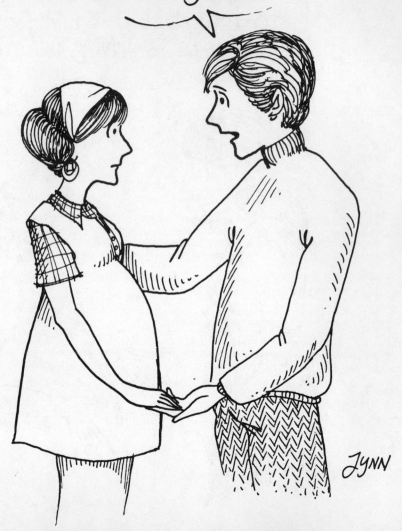

79

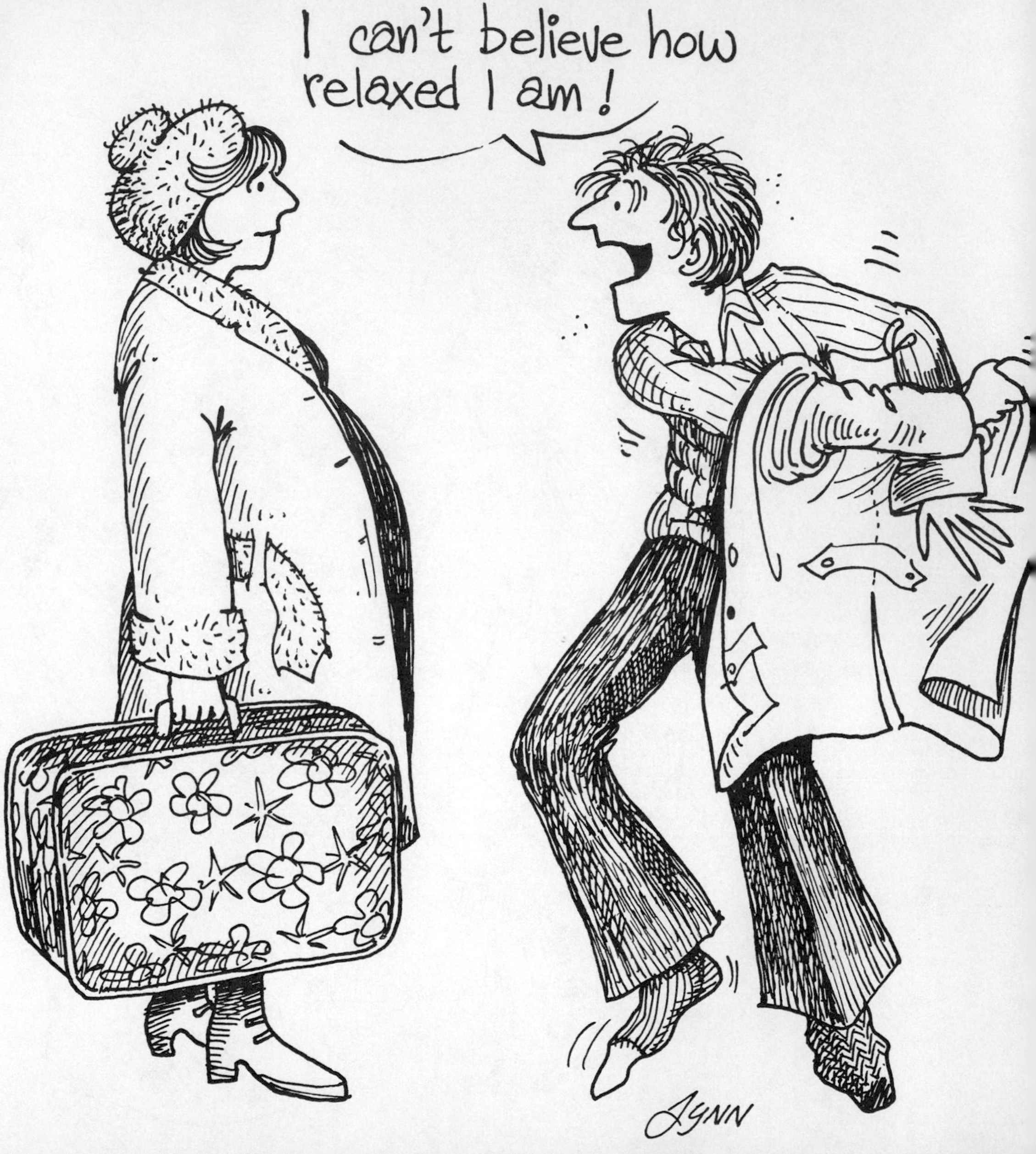
I can't believe how relaxed I am!
LYNN

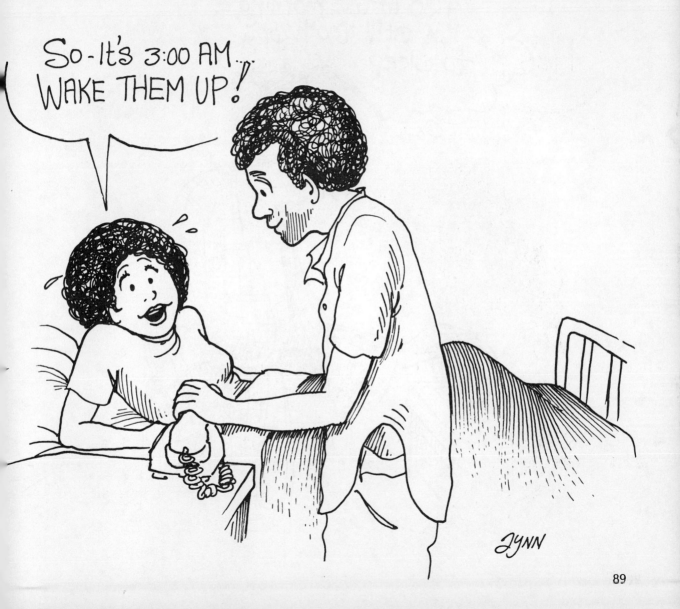

97

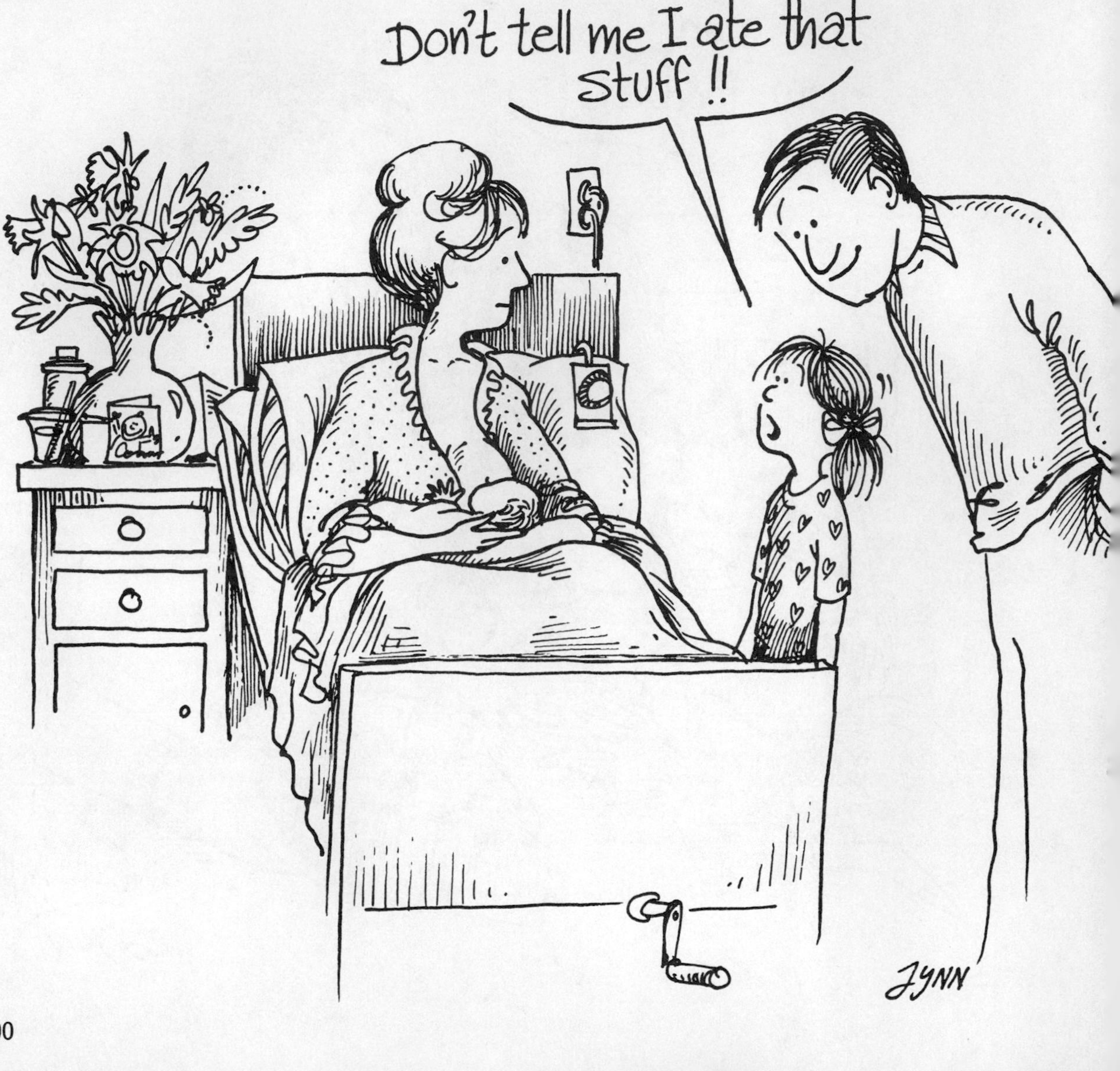
Don't tell me I ate that stuff !!

103

107

Meet Lynn Johnston

Lynn Johnston is North America's best-selling female cartoonist. She draws much of her material from close observation of her family: Aaron, Katie and husband Rod (a dentist). Lynn's deft, humorous depictions of life with kids have provided her with material for three books published by Meadowbrook, plus an internationally syndicated comic strip, "For Better Or For Worse." Lynn and her family live in Corbeil, Ontario.

& Her Books:

DAVID WE'RE PREGNANT!!

101 laughing out loud cartoons that accentuate the humorous side of conceiving, expecting and giving birth. A great baby shower gift, it's the perfect way to bolster the spirits of any expectant couple.

Meadowbrook Ordering #1049 $3.95

HI MOM! HI DAD!

A side splitting sequel to DAVID WE'RE PREGNANT! 101 cartoons on the first year of childrearing . . . . .all those late night wakings, early morning wakings, and other traumatic "emergencies" too numerous to list.

Meadowbrook Ordering #1139 $3.95

DO THEY EVER GROW UP?

This third in her series of cartoon books is a hilarious survival guide for parents of the tantrum and pacifier set, as well as a side splitting memory book for parents who have lived through it.

Meadowbrook Ordering #1089 $3.95

Parenting Books

Our Baby's First Year

A Baby Record Calendar
A nursery calendar with 13 undated months for recording "big events" of baby's first year. Each month features animal characters, and baby care and development tips. Photo album page and family tree, too! A great shower gift!

Meadowbrook Ordering #3179 $8.95

Parents' Guide to Baby & Child Medical Care

by Terril H. Hart, M.D.

A first aid and home treatment guide that shows parents how to handle over 150 common childhood illnesses in a step-by-step illustrated format. Includes a symptoms index, health record forms, child-proofing tips, and more.

Meadowbrook Ordering #1159 $5.95

Grandma Knows Best But No One Ever Listens

by Mary McBride

Mary McBride instructs grandmas who have been stuck with baby-sitting how to "scheme, lie, cheat, and threaten so you'll be thought of as a sweet, darling grandma."

Meadowbrook Ordering #: 4009 $4.95

Mother Murphy's Law

by Bruce Lansky

The wit of Bombeck and the wisdom of Murphy are combined in this collection of 325 laws that detail the perils and pitfalls of parenthood. Cartoon illustrations by Christine Tripp.

Meadowbrook Ordering #1149 $2.95

ORDER FORM

Order #	Qty.	Book Title	Author	Price
1159	____	Baby and Child Medical Care	Hart, T.	$ 5.95
1039	____	Baby Talk	Lansky, B.	$ 4.95
1029	____	Best Baby Name Book, The	Lansky, B.	$ 3.95
1049	____	David, We're Pregnant!	Johnston, L.	$ 3.95
1059	____	Dear Babysitter	Lansky, V.	$ 8.95
1069	____	Dear Babysitter Refill Pad	Lansky, V.	$ 2.50
1079	____	Discipline Without Shouting or Spanking	Wyckoff/Unell	$ 4.95
1089	____	Do They Ever Grow Up?	Johnston, L.	$ 3.95
1099	____	Exercises for Baby and Me	Regnier, S.	$ 8.95
1109	____	Feed Me! I'm Yours	Lansky, V.	$ 6.95
1119	____	First Year Baby Care	Kelly, P.	$ 5.95
2190	____	Free Stuff for Kids	FSFK Editors	$ 3.95
3109	____	Grandma's Favorites Photo Album	Meadowbrook	$ 6.50
4009	____	Grandma Knows Best	McBride, M.	$ 4.95
1139	____	Hi Mom! Hi Dad!	Johnston, L.	$ 3.95
1149	____	Mother Murphy's Law	Lansky, B.	$ 2.95
3129	____	My First Five Years Record Book	Meadowbrook	$12.95
3119	____	My First Year Calendar	Meadowbrook	$ 7.95
3139	____	My First Year Photo Album	Meadowbrook	$14.95
3179	____	Our Baby's First Year Calendar	Meadowbrook	$ 8.95
1179	____	Practical Parenting Tips	Lansky, V.	$ 6.95
1169	____	Pregnancy, Childbirth and the Newborn	Simkin/Whalley	$ 9.95
1199	____	Successful Breastfeeding	Dana/Price	$ 8.95

Please send me copies of the books checked above. I am enclosing $_____ (full amount per each copy and $1.25 for first copy and $.50 for each additional copy to cover postage and handling. Order to be sent to Canada add $2.00 for extra postage. Overseas postage and handling will be billed). **Quantity discounts on request.** Allow up to four weeks for delivery.

Send check or money order to Meadowbrook, Inc. No cash or C.O.D.s, please.

Mail order to: Book Orders
Meadowbrook, Inc.
18318 Minnetonka Blvd.
Deephaven, MN 55391

Phone orders: (612) 473-5400
or (800) 338-2232

For purchases over $10.00, you may use VISA or MasterCard (order by mail or phone). For these orders we need information below.

Charge to: ☐ **VISA** ☐ **MasterCard**

Account #_____

Expiration Date_____

Card Signature_____

Send Book(s) to:

Name_____

Address_____

City_____State_____Zip_____